Extensions of Love

A Play

by

Darren Rapier

Based on an original concept by Stuart Murdoch

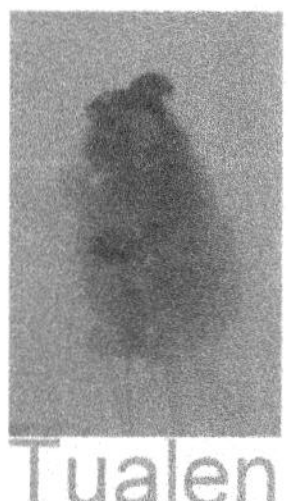

Tualen Press
PO Box 239
Sidcup
DA16 0DP
United Kingdom
info@spannerintheworks.org.uk

First Published 2011

For performance rights of this play please contact:

Andrew Mann Ltd.,
1 Old Compton Street,
London, W1D 5JA
Tel: 020 7734 4751
Fax: 020 7287 9264
info@andrewmann.co.uk

SETTING

The play takes place present day in two London apartments.
The definition between the apartments is not clear on the stage.
Throughout the performance AMANDA gradually takes more and more of the space, forcing LENA into a corner both physically and mentally.
Scenes are marked as those in which the main action takes place, however there may be subdued action going on at the same time in the other flat.

SOUNDS

Sounds are very important. All the tones, clicks, footsteps, messages are played over the PA. They increase in intensity as the play progresses.

BRIEF CHARACTER BIOGRAPHIES

LENA KERN

(**Lena** : LAY-nuh : Latin "temptress"/ **Kern** : KURN : Gaelic "dark")

Is a successful and attractive marketing manager at a small firm in London, producing 'in-house' magazines and newsletters for prestigious blue chip companies. She bought into the firm early on and has continued to contribute to their mutual success ever since. She is outgoing and likeable and has a busy social life. But her job is not nine to five. Often she is working to a deadline for international clients and will have to have calls, faxes and emails re-directed to her home or mobile phone. Because of the nature of her work it is important that she gets on with people. There are people both in her company and contacts outside who will know her name and phone number, that she may have only met once, or not at all face to face. Over the years she has also got to know some of her clients and suppliers, photographers etc. very well. She enjoys flirting with them, as they do with her, which is inevitably part of her success. She has been seeing her current boyfriend GREG for about three months and she is already getting bored with him.

AMANDA JUDD

(**Amanda** : AH-man-dah : latin "worthy of love"/ **Judd** : JUD : Hebrew "praised")

Lives alone, on a housing estate in Kennington. She works as a secretary, temping for an agency to earn a living. The job frustrates her as she has a good, bordering on photographic, memory and so every little quip she is the butt of she remembers. She is frugal with her money although she does not go without. Once she has decided to buy something she will spend hours deciding exactly which item it will be, researching, testing and searching for the precise article. She is doing a correspondence course in classics, however this is very much a labour of love. Once she has discovered a text, or a piece of music or poetry she will delve deeper and deeper in to find out every last detail. Consequently she rarely gets time to write up the assignments as she is too busy reading. She is passionately romantic, but finds most people far too shallow to allow them close to her.

'Love is, above all, the gift of oneself'

Jean Anouilh

EXTENSIONS OF LOVE was first presented by Undiscovered Productions at The Oval House Theatre on 9th October 2002 with the following cast:

Lena Kern .... Marielle Dreier
Amanda Judd .... Catherine Carolan

Set Design ....Kate Bannister & Karl Swinyard
Lighting Design .... Stuart Gain
Sound Design .... Leon Benning

Directed by Stuart Murdoch

EXTENSIONS OF LOVE

By Darren Rapier

Based on an original concept by Stuart Murdoch

SCENE ONE: BOTH FLATS, SUMMER – DAY.

A PHONE rings somewhere in the auditorium. Loud enough to hear, to want to answer, but it keeps on ringing until the audience are seated. When it stops ***AMANDA*** *and* ***LENA*** *present their speeches straight to the audience, as if they have just been asked the question 'What is love?' by a stranger interviewing people on the street.*

LENA: What is love? Love is an affliction. It's something that catches you off guard, like a barbed hook, hiding in the murky waters. It's often one sided, or maybe it just seems that way. I don't think anyone can force you to love them, it just happens. It's such a bizarre concept, this 'mystical' attachment. It screws you up, definitely, there are far too many distractions in life. That's why you need to stay in control, that's essential I think - focus on what's important. Life is too short to let anything cloud your vision, so you have to keep your head, keep reminding yourself of your goals. Without that you're lost – a victim of your own emotions.

AMANDA: Love is obsessive. It envelops you, consuming your whole life. There's no choice: You fall in to this fast flowing river, carried along, rushing past while life on the shady banks is a blur of mundane pointless tasks. It's all there is. Everything that's gone before is swept away in the torrent of emotion. It occupies every waking hour. While you might try to ignore it, fight it, reason with it... It's there, clawing at the door, waiting for you to discover that there is nothing as strong, nothing as enduring, nothing as overwhelming. And when you're struck, struck by that poison tipped arrow, well it's hopeless. You can't fight that: Submission is the only choice. That's the truth of it.

They both turn and exit out of their respective doors.

MUSIC: Jazz, busy. As...

SCENE TWO: <u>BOTH FLATS, CHANGING SEASONS - DAY/NIGHT.</u>

They re-enter, in their outdoor clothes. As the two women run through their everyday ritualistic routines of coming in and going out, repeating them several times over, it is the music we hear, not their voices or actions. The audience should feel like voyeurs, peeping in on their mundane lives. Their routines include how and where they put their keys down, what their priorities are: Taking off and putting on shoes and coats, putting down bags, putting on music, washing hands, putting out the rubbish, reading the post, going to the toilet – whatever they think of when first entering or when just leaving their own private space.

AMANDA's tasks include putting out food for the cat and pouring herself a glass of wine. It is apparent she lives alone, that her flat is a large and important part of her life, she rarely goes out. She is careful and methodical in what she does.

LENA on the other hand is chaotic. Her clothes are strewn about, she checks her messages while putting on her shoes to go out, she checks her emails while brushing her teeth, she is constantly on the phone. Her life is busy, her flat is merely a place to stay.

As the time passes, perhaps unnoticed, AMANDA removes the cat's objects from the flat. She becomes even more self contained and alone.

LENA is always checking post, messages and email, she likes to be contactable.

Eventually they both exit independently from their own flats.

The MUSIC stops suddenly as...

SCENE THREE: AMANDA'S FLAT, SPRING – DAY.

The door to AMANDA's flat opens suddenly and AMANDA and LENA burst in. LENA is flustered, perhaps a little bewildered, she is holding her face, the victim of an attack. AMANDA is concerned and reassuring. There is an air of confusion.

LENA: ...Little bastard!

AMANDA: Here, let me...

LENA winces, as AMANDA tries to touch her face.

AMANDA: Give me these.

She takes LENA's bags from her. LENA looks out of the door, before AMANDA returns and gently guides her into the flat.

AMANDA: He'll be long gone by now...

AMANDA looks out of the door, before closing it.

LENA: I didn't even see where he came from...

AMANDA: Here, let me see...

LENA: It's fine, honestly...

AMANDA: Would you like to...?

LENA: I'm OK, really... (*She flexes her cheek*) Ouch.

AMANDA: Perhaps some ice, or something...?

LENA continues flexing her face.

AMANDA: A drink?

LENA: Maybe a steak?

AMANDA: ?

LENA: Isn't that good for a black eye?

AMANDA: (*Relived*) Oh. I might have a couple of chicken pieces?

LENA: Do you have a phone I could borrow?

AMANDA: Of course, it's erm...

She indicates the phone.

AMANDA: (*Referring to her face*) You should probably get someone to have a look at that.

LENA: It's just a bit... How old do you reckon he was?

AMANDA: I don't know, thirteen/ fourteen?

LENA starts to rummage through her bag.

AMANDA: Would you like a drink?

LENA: No..., Thanks.

AMANDA: A tea perhaps?

LENA: (*Dialling*) Honestly, I'm fine.

AMANDA: I think tea is good, isn't it? For shock.

LENA shakes her head as her call connects. AMANDA stands, watching her, unsure whether to make a drink or not .

LENA: Yes ... Andrew? Some little bastard stole my phone ... yes ... yes, just ripped it out of my hand ... so I can't ... no, no, I'm OK. It's just ... exactly ... punched me in the face, no, no ... someone's done the rescue thing, I'm fine, really. No, I didn't just get fed up with talking ... I'd .... you spoke to him? Well.., what did he? Cheek! Twelve/thirteen ... Yeah, Look I'll talk to you when I get back to the office ... Don't be ridiculous it would take more than one spotty teenager. Yeah, thanks, bye.

She places the phone down, but immediately picks it up again and dials. AMANDA watches her, unsure of what to do.

LENA: (*To AMANDA*) He spoke to him, can you believe it? Told him I was 'fixing my face'. I tell you... (*The call connects*) Listen to me you little piece of shit, how dare you think you can go... Hello, hello!

LENA slams down the phone, much to AMANDA's surprise. Then she realises what she has done.

LENA: Oh, I'm so sorry. Erm.

AMANDA: (*Slightly put out*) Don't worry.

LENA: That's not me, I... I didn't know what else to do. I'm so annoyed.

AMANDA: You're probably a bit shocked. Let me get that drink.

LENA: I'm really sorry about this, dragging you into... Well, you've been very kind.

As AMANDA gets the drink LENA presses re-dial. She listens for a minute before...

LENA: (*To AMANDA*) He's switched it off. At least he won't be able to make any more calls on it without my pin number. (*She waits to leave a message. The adrenalin has subsided*). This is my stolen phone, hopefully I'll get this message later.

AMANDA: It's hardly your fault is it?

LENA: Always thought I'd be a bit more prepared somehow...

AMANDA: (*Handing her the drink)* Here.

LENA: (*Pause*) Would you mind if I just made one more call? I'll be as quick as I can.

AMANDA: Of course.

LENA puts down her drink and takes her diary out of her bag. It is full of bits of paper, every page is scrawled with things to do - chaotic. She opens the address page and takes out a little card. As AMANDA watches in silence she dials the number.

LENA: Hello, yes I've just had my phone stolen and I'd like to transfer all the calls. Yes, it's 07858 426871. Kern, Lena Kern. SE1 7PQ. Archer. Yes. About ten/fifteen minutes ago. Yes, my home phone? Yes. It's 020 7361 3484. Yes. And how soon can I ... Yes, can I phone you back because I'm on someone else's phone. Yep, about half an hour? Lucy? OK, thank you.

She puts the phone down gently.

AMANDA: Hadn't you better phone the police? I don't mind, really.

LENA: No, I don't think so. What are they going to do? Unless we knew where he lived.

LENA goes to put the Filofax back into her bag, when she flicks through it.

LENA: I hope I've got all those numbers in here?

AMANDA: You need a secretary.

LENA: I've got one. Imagine what I'd be like without him.

AMANDA: Are you going to be alright?

LENA: Like I said, it's more annoying than anything. Sorry I haven't even... I'm Lena.

AMANDA: So I heard. I'm Amanda, Amanda Judd.

LENA: I'm normally good with faces, but I couldn't even tell you the colour of his hair.

AMANDA: It's probably best to forget about it, just get on with things.

LENA: (*Rubbing her face again*) He's left me with a nice reminder though.

She starts to walk towards the door.

AMANDA: Are you sure you'll be alright?

LENA: Yes. Thanks Amanda.

She gives AMANDA's arm a gentle squeeze in gratitude, then opens the door.

LENA: Look out for yourself next time you're using your mobile.

AMANDA: Oh, I don't actually...

They exchange a smile and LENA exits.

AMANDA gives a feeble wave and closes the door, she presses her back against it and looks into the room.

SCENE FOUR: LENA'S FLAT, SPRING – DAY.

LENA is getting ready to go out, she is just checking her emails, as she eats a piece of toast. Two wine glasses sit on the table, clothes are strewn all over the place.
A SHOWER can be heard running in the bathroom (off), along with FIRE STARTER by Prodigy playing and perhaps the occasional accompaniment by GREG (off).
LENA clicks at the mouse, reading the emails as she speaks.

LENA: (*Calling towards the bathroom*) ...Come on, we should have left five minutes ago! It won't be a 'who done it', as much as a 'what was it they did' at this rate.

She pours herself another glass of wine and takes a bite of toast. One of the emails from work seems to annoy her slightly.

LENA: (*To herself*) What is the matter with these people?

Lena turns off the computer and picks up the phone, she calls to GREG as she dials. With the phone at her ear she sorts through the days post. As she is speaking she is constantly skimming letters then Placing them in three piles on the table: Letters to keep, Letters/envelopes to throw away and non recyclable rubbish.

LENA: (*To Greg*) Could you turn that down a bit? Greg! (*The phone connects*). Hello, Andrew? Glad I caught you, I knew you'd be burning the midnight. Could you do me a favour? I'm on my way out, but I've just got an email from Steve and he might want to talk to me before his meeting ... .. I don't know, but they're ten hours ahead, so he's bound to be asleep by now, so could you transfer my calls here? .... No home, I'm going to a dinner party, if we ever leave that is ... .. Yes, it's a sort of a 'murder mystery' thing. You know what they're like, if you miss the crucial clue at the beginning, ...Yeah I will, thanks. See you.

She puts the phone down, sighs towards the direction of the bathroom, then throws the paper rubbish in the recycling bin and the rest in the regular bin. She puts her watch on and looks at the time.

LENA: (*Calling*) Come on Greg, you must have washed your skin off by now! That's not personal hygiene, it's an obsessive disorder. (*To herself*) With any luck it'll be you they're murdering this evening.

She exits.

SCENE FIVE: AMANDA'S FLAT, SPRING – DAY.

AMANDA sits quiet and alone in her flat, reading the poetry of Charles Baudelaire (The Flowers of Evil). On the Hi-Fi SHOSTAKOVICH – Cello Concertos, No. 1 in E flat Major, No. 2 in G Major plays.
She is totally absorbed in her own world.
She hears a noise at the door, she sits up and turns down the stereo. She listens intently.
She turns off the stereo and goes to the spy hole and looks out. She stays there for ages, studying the world outside.
Eventually she returns to her seat, but as she passes the phone she strokes it fondly. She settles herself down and starts the CD again, turning it to a comfortable volume. She opens her book.
The PHONE RINGS.
AMANDA looks at it for a moment, then she carefully closes her book and pauses the CD. She gathers herself and walks over to the phone. She answers it.

AMANDA: Hello? ... Oh, it's you. No, no, I was just ... , just sorting some things out. No, no I haven't heard anything about him. I.., I have tried. I have tried mother, what do you expect me to do? Yes, yes I have. No, I don't think so, I've stopped putting food out for him now .... No I'm not putting posters up, I don't want to advertise my phone number on every lamp post around here .... Work? How can I, it changes every week, sometimes every day. Perhaps I should put the agency number? ... No, it was a joke. They're not the RSPCA are they? ... I've looked everywhere.... Someone else? Maybe, how should I know? No, no I'm not going to replace him..., it's too much of a tie, you know? ... Look, mother I..., no listen I'm a bit busy at the moment.... Yes, yes I'm trying to finish an essay, for my course, yes.... Well, I keep getting..., yes I'm half way through writing it now.... Sorting? Yes, that's what I meant..., I've got my books out all over the floor... (*She looks guiltily at the empty floor*) It's, well you wouldn't understand, it's... Greek, yes, literally. Who?... Well you wouldn't... Yes it's, who? Apollo and Daphne, you... it would take too long mother... I really... I should get back to it. No, no not for a while, it's not like taking your GCSE's. Yes, yes I will... I will, yes, I said I would. Yes, yes OK, yes, yes, I really must... yes, goodbye. OK, goodbye.

She places the receiver down slowly, irritated by the interruption. She looks at the phone for a few moments, grinding her teeth slightly. She goes to lift the receiver, but doesn't. Taking a deep breath she walks over and picks up a large folder – a correspondence course in classics. She looks at it, weighs it in her hands then places it back. She exhales, as if recovering from an anxiety attack, then turns the CD player back on. Slowly she relaxes, then settles back on the sofa and opens the book,

SCENE SIX: LENA'S FLAT, SPRING – NIGHT.

LENA's phone is ringing.
Her KEY CAN BE HEARD in the door (Off). The exterior door is heard OPENING.

LENA: *(Off, calling)* The phone's ringing. Phone! I'll see you in a minute.

She blunders in, slightly drunk and totters over to the phone.

LENA: Lena Kern, hello?

SOFT CLICK, followed by DIALLING TONE.

LENA: Shit.

She puts down the receiver and starts back to the door to open it for GREG, but as she gets to the door the PHONE rings again. She turns and snatches it up.

LENA: (Agitated) Lena Kern... *(Then relaxed, flirting slightly)* Patrick. No, not at all I've only just come in.... No, with Greg, he's parking the car.... No, he's still around thank you.... I'm sure I don't know what you mean. All of three months... Hardly. Anyway, why are you phoning me at this unearthly hour?.... Oh, and there's me thinking you just wanted to hear my voice. They're working you too hard at that place. ... Yes, you should come over to us as a contract, I'd put in a good word for you. (*She laughs*) Just a minute, let me get my diary.

She reaches over and gets out her diary, as before it is stuffed with bits of paper, chaotic.

LENA: Right. When are we looking at? *(She flicks through the pages)* Erm..., can't do that darling, far too busy.... Tuesday? Let me see..., it's a possibility. If I could make head or tail of this, I think twelve-thirty might be a possibility? (*Reading*) It's flair...? Hair! Hair, but I can change that – no problem.... For you darling, anything's possible. ... Good. How does twelve-thirty sound?

The DOOR BELL rings.

LENA: Oh, it's Greg. Can you hang on a minute?... I thought you said you'd wait as long as it took? Oh, I see, I've got competition now have I?

DOOR BELL rings again, twice.

LENA: (*Calling*) Hang on! (*Then back to* phone) Alright, Tuesday it is, you can buy me lunch. Bloody cheek, I'm the client here you know. Well then I'm the client's agent, and that means you have to buy me lunch. Bring the photos.... No, for the magazine darling, for the magazine. And bring your platinum credit card, you'll need it. (*She* laughs) See you Tuesday Patrick.

DOOR BELL rings again, over and over.
LENA places the phone down. Her jovial mood is wiped off almost straight away, as she looks over to the door and shakes her head in annoyance. She strides over to the door, opens it and goes out to the main door.

LENA (*Leaving*): I was on the bloody phone, are you deaf?

SCENE SEVEN: AMANDA'S FLAT, SPRING – EARLY EVENING.

AMANDA enters her flat, she goes though her routine. She makes herself a sandwich and takes it to the sofa.. She looks at the poetry book but is too distracted to read it. She looks around the empty flat.
She sees something poking out of the cushion. She pulls it out, discovering it is a little stuffed mouse - the last cat toy. She passes it playfully from hand to hand for a moment before standing up and throwing it into the bin. She is all alone now, the outside world beyond the peep hole. She walks over to the peep hole and looks out.
She goes and picks up her sandwich, collecting a chair on her way back to the door. She sits at the peep hole, staring out and eating her sandwich.

SCENE EIGHT: LENA'S FLAT, SUMMER – MORNING.

LENA is shouting over the sound of her HAIRDRYER.

LENA: (*Off*) I thought you said you'd take me in? I'm going to be late now. Yeah, well I assumed you'd have got out of bed in the mean time! No, don't bother getting up off your fat arse. Oh forget it!

BEDROOM DOOR SLAMS off.
Beat.
LENA enters the room, fuming, she has the post in her hand as she grabs her work bag from beside the sofa. She glances at the letters, one catches her eye. She looks at her watch, but she is already late. Throwing the other letters on the desk she opens the one that has caught her eye – complementary tickets to the opera.

LENA (*To herself*): Awe, Carmen, Patrick you sweety.

The SHOWER starts to run, off.
LENA shoots a disdainful look.

LENA: Don't think you're going to be coming with me, you lazy git.

She tucks the tickets into her pocket, picks up her keys and exits.

SCENE NINE: AMANDA'S FLAT, SUMMER - EARLY EVENING

AMANDA enters her flat, she starts her routine but there is a tension in her actions. She gradually seems to be getting more agitated, annoyed. The pressure builds and builds until, unable to contain herself any longer she throws herself onto her hands and knees in despair.

AMANDA: (*Wailing*) What's the point! What's the fucking point! I have to deal with this crap, I don't have to deal with it. Why should I? Why should I have to deal with it? 'If you can't deal with it, then perhaps you're not in the right job?' Of course I'm not in the right job you stupid bitch. What possible pleasure could I get from being some office lackey to a bunch of uncultured Neanderthal pricks!? Do you think I actually enjoy your company? Do you think I would choose to inhabit the same breathing space as such a sack load of shit!? (*She wipes the tears from her* face) I didn't want this, I didn't want to be doing this. There is more to life than your petty office politics. I just, just... I deserve more than this. I deserve more than this. Look at this place. What does any of it matter?

She stands and goes to get herself a drink. There is an empty glass on the side, but she doesn't use it, she takes a new one.

AMANDA: Those..., how dare they. How dare they? Pieces of paper for Christ's sake. What possible difference could it make? What possible difference could a hundred pieces of paper make to anyone? And they... they... I know what I was told. I know, because I don't forget. Not like some people. 'Twenty-five, forty-seven, fifty-three, eighty-six, eighty-eight and ninety'. 'Twenty-three copies of each' – there. Oh I bet they're having a laugh at the agency, a good laugh on me. How dare you tell me it was my mistake. Twenty-three copies - Twenty-five, forty-seven, fifty-three, eighty-six, eighty-eight and ninety. There's nothing wrong with my memory. I don't have to work for these people, I don't have to take this crap every day from those bitches. And the agency's in on it, they think it's some bloody big bastard joke, just like the bitches at the office. A big bloody joke on Amanda Judd. Well they can fuck off! The lot of them.

She rummages through a stack of papers and pulls out a local newspaper. Still sniffing she sits down and starts to look through it.

AMANDA: There's plenty more fish in the sea. Plenty more. All these agencies to choose from, why do I always choose the wrong one? They're just names. Thousands and thousands of names, but which one? How can you tell anything...?

She stops and looks over at the phone.
SOFT CLICKS, like Morse code.
She is still looking over at the phone – is this where they are coming from?
She listens intently. Gradually she seems to understand them, recognising them as a message, which somehow comforts her.
She stands and wipes her eyes, moving slowly to the phone.
Cautiously she picks it up.
SOFT DIALLING TONE, the CLICKS STOP dead.
AMANDA listens to the tone for a moment, before putting the receiver down slowly.

AMANDA: No. I must sort this out on my own.

She walks over and pours herself another drink.

SOFT CLICKS.

A gentle smiles plays on her lips as she looks across the room to the phone.

AMANDA: (*Towards the phone, fondly*) I can't expect you to fight my battles for me. I have my own life to live.

The SOFT CLICKS continue as...

SCENE TEN: LENA'S FLAT, SUMMER – EVENING.

LENA clicks the mouse on her PC as she check her emails.
FADE UP MUSIC from LENA's Hi-Fi: 'SOUL SURFING' – by Fat Boy Slim.
She is alone in her flat for the first time that we have seen, but she hardly seems to notice.
She turns off the PC and picks up the TV remote. Flicking it on she skips through a few channels before deciding there is nothing to watch and switching it off.
She starts to tidy up half heartedly.
The PHONE RINGS, saving her. She dashes over to pick it up..

LENA: Lena Kern. Alicia? ... How's things? Good. No, I'm at home, Greg's away this week. ... Still manically busy, what about you? ... Are you still seeing Cliff, Clive? Whatever his name is. Oh, sorry. ... Nothing, nothing at all. ... OK, what time? ... Great. ...Nine thirty? Shall I meet you there? Leicester Square, yep? Excellent, see you later, bye.

She puts down the phone and looks at her watch - hours to go yet.
She looks around the flat, at a loss with herself. A copy of a trashy novel lies, bent back open on the sofa. She picks it up and glances down the page. With no alternative this is what she decides she will do. She sits on the sofa and starts to read.
MUSIC FADES to CLICKS, SLIGHTLY LOUDER.

SCENE ELEVEN: AMANDA'S FLAT, SUMMER – EVENING.

CLICKS STOP.
AMANDA enters her flat. She goes through the ritual that she has every day. She takes out a CD, cleans it and puts it on. She pours herself a glass of wine and relaxes. She takes out a writing pad and writes, speaking aloud as she composes a love letter.

AMANDA: 'My Darling, thank you for your message the other day, I really don't know how I could have coped if it wasn't for your encouragement and kindness. I now find myself in happier circumstances. You have been in my thoughts for days now, everywhere I look I see your face, I find myself yearning to be with you, impossible as it is. I have no desire to embark in these fantasies of love, although desire is somehow all I have. If we are careful, if we can suppress the urge to shout out love from the highest rooftop, no one need ever know but us. I am both excited and frightened by the prospect, as I have never done anything like this before. I follow your lead, I look forward to your reply with eagerness and anticipation.'

She folds the letter carefully and places it into the envelope. Turning it over she writes the addressee's name on the front. She pauses for a moment, ruminating...

AMANDA: SE1 7PQ.

She writes the postcode on the front of the envelope, seals it and then crosses the room, walking right through LENA's space. She drops it in LENA's flat, in front of the door.

SCENE TWELVE: LENA'S FLAT, SUMMER – EARLY EVENING.

LENA enters she goes through her ritualistic routine. She checks the answerphone as she looks through the post.

ANSWERPHONE (VO): You have nine new messages...

There are VARIOUS MESSAGES both business and personal, one from ALICIA telling her they are going out tomorrow to a club, two CLICKS of the receiver after a short pause. The messages continue as...
She comes to AMANDA's letter, she is puzzled as it has a name and postcode only.
She unfolds the letter and reads it as...

GREG (VO): (*ANSWERPHONE*) Yeah, Lena? It's Greg. Pick up if you're there hun. Lena? OK, it's five-thirty and I'm just ringing to say I can't make it tonight. Sorry it's such late notice but Barry's got something on and..., look I'll call your mobile OK? Maybe we can hook up later in the week? I'll make it up to you, I promise.

She narrows her eyes at the message, then looks back at the letter. There are a couple of messages before the answerphone switches off as...
LENA (reading) grins to herself, someone wants her. She places the letter on the side and pours herself a drink, wondering who her secret admirer is.

SCENE THIRTEEN: AMANDA'S FLAT, SUMMER – MORNING.

AMANDA waits by the door with her coat on and her bag over her shoulder, ready to leave. She is transfixed by the letterbox, almost in a state of suspended animation. The mail comes through the door and she rushes to collect it. She flicks through it, but seems frustrated that there is something missing. She opens one plain envelope but is again disappointed. Throwing it down she paces the floor, clutching her mouth, thinking. She goes over to the phone and picks it up.

SOFT DIALLING TONE, then CLICK to connection.

AMANDA: Hello? Yes, erm, this is Amanda Judd... Judd. Yes, I'm sorry but I won't be able to make it in today... No, something's come up I... Well it's unexpected, a personal matter. No, no tomorrow should be fine. Yes, I realise it's late notice, but... No, it won't happen again. Goodbye.

She pauses for a moment, she seems uncertain, a little lost.
SOFT CLICKS.
AMANDA gently covers her ears, still looking at the phone. She waits as the CLICKS GROW LOUDER. She cannot resist it any more, she picks up the receiver and dials.
THE CLICKS STOP, THE PHONE CONNECTS, FAINT RINGING.
RINGS STOP, as the phone connects.
AMANDA waits, while the message plays (unheard). She goes to speak after she has heard the tone, and nearly does so, but she can't bring herself to do it. She puts the phone down.
Not knowing what to do she paces up and down a few times, before sitting down and taking out the pad.
She takes out the Boudelaire book and places it onto the sofa beside her.
She sits and writes, continuing as...

SCENE FOURTEEN: LENA'S FLAT, SUMMER – EVENING.

LENA enters, she is carrying some paper rubbish in a bag which has split open. She is preoccupied by the paper spilling out, some of which has blown down the street outside.

LENA: Bloody kids.

She kicks the mail on the way in, scattering it across the floor. Clearly aggravated by the whole thing she brings the bag in and Selotapes it up.
Dusting off her hands she goes through her ritualistic routine.

ANSWERPHONE (VO): You have thirteen new messages...

The ANSWERPHONE MESSAGES PLAY, SLIGHTLY LOUDER. There are MORE of them that are simply the PHONE BEING PUT DOWN, among all the others. Some of these have LONGER GAPS.

As she flicks through the post she notices that there are three letters in the same envelopes as before.
The PHONE RINGS, she picks it up straight away.

LENA: Lena Kern. Oh, hi Alicia. Sorry I didn't get a chance to call you back earlier. ... Tonight? Yeah, great. ... No I haven't eaten, so that's fine. Hey, guess what? I think I've got a secret admirer. ... Yes, he's sending me romantic letters. ... Greg? You must be joking. ... I'm not reading them to you, they're private. ... No. It's between me and my admirer. ... No, I haven't any idea. Well there's so many, you know? (*She laughs*) Probably someone having a laugh. ... No, no gifts, I'm a bit disappointed about that. ... No, I' not going to bring them. See you there at eight - unless I get a better offer. ... Yeah, bye.

LENA returns to the letters. Curiously she opens the first one. She reads as...

AMANDA (READING): 'I have been waiting, for what seems an eternity, to hear your reply. I can only assume that things have been too busy, or he has been looking over your shoulder at every opportunity you've had. If the former is the case, darling please take care of yourself, it's not good for you to work so hard. Sometimes people will have to wait, like I am prepared to do...'

LENA stops reading, she looks up from the page.
She starts to read again.

AMANDA (READING): '...Like I am prepared to do, we can't all expect everything right away.
If it is the latter – and he dogging your every move – darling perhaps the time has come to tell him. I know, I know you'll say it is too early, that's your nature – to be kind to others. But surely it is better to tell him now than to keep him hanging on when really we both know all hope is lost. You really need to think more of yourself, you're worth...'

LENA puts the letter down. She is trying to decide if it is a joke.
She looks at it cautiously, then to the other two.
She opens the second letter and starts to read...

AMANDA (READING): 'I tried to call again today, but as ever you were out...'

LENA stops and looks over at the answerphone. She continues.

AMANDA (READING): '...You should try to allocate your time better, I am beside myself with worry sometimes. I'm sure that you have been very busy and console myself with the thought that this is the reason I still haven't heard from you. I was reading this today and thought of you:
"Imagine how sweet
To live there as lovers do!
To kiss as we choose
To love and to die..." '

LENA puts down the letter, slightly unnerved by it. She doesn't want to read any more, but her curiosity draws her to the third letter. After a short pause she opens it. Slowly unfolding it she reads...

AMANDA (READING): 'My darling, I am sitting here awaiting your response. I have not been able to go to work today as I have been so worried about you. I know you would think me silly for fretting like this, but I needed to be sure you are alright. I feel like I am imprisoned by the passion to be with you, held captive by the fact that if I dare leave this room I will be compelled to see you, just a glimpse to reassure myself that you are OK. Yet I know that one glimpse would not be enough. Like Narcissus drawn to the waters edge I would be suck fast, transfixed by such beauty that...'

The PHONE RINGS LOUDLY, causing LENA to jump.

LENA: Lena Kern... (*Pause*). Hello?... Hello, who is this?

The PHONE CUTS OFF, SOFT DIALLING TONE.

LENA waits for a moment. She looks back at the letters. She puts the phone down and dials 1,4,7,1.

OPERATOR (VO): You were called today at nineteen-forty-three hours. The caller withheld their number.

LENA looks back at the letters. She picks up the last one and reads...

AMANDA (READING): '...Transfixed by such beauty that I would not be able to pull myself away. My situation is hopeless without you. Your messages are of some comfort but you cannot expect me to keep phoning and writing like this. You have to take time, as I have, to put work aside for a moment and think about what's important to you...'

LENA puts down the letter. She thinks for a moment, then she picks up the first letter and scans the page...

AMANDA (READING): '...Sometimes people will have to wait, like I am prepared to do...'

LENA smiles. There is a sense of relief. She takes her Filofax out of her bag and looks up a phone number. She dials.

LENA: (*Jolly*) Hello, Patrick?... Fine thanks, how are you?... Surprise, really? No, I was just phoning to say thanks for the letters. It took me a while but... The letters? (*Her confidence is slightly dented*) The erm... Yes, the... Oh, what am I talking about? The confirmation, yes. I've had a busy day.... (*She tries to recover her* composure) At home? I'm out all day tomorrow, so I thought I'd catch you this evening. Just wanted to hear your voice, yes.... Don't flatter yourself darling... You know me, never stop working... Yes, I'll look forward to it. Have a nice evening... Yes, bye. See you.

She places the phone down and looks at the letters, the sense of unease returns.

Decisively she snatches them up, screwing them all together. She marches over to the bin bag full of paper and stuffs them in. Looking around she picks up the other letter she had saved and throws that away also. She puts the bin bag out of sight, shakes the incident from her mind and returns to her routine.

SCENE FIFTEEN: AMANDA'S FLAT, SUMMER – DAY.

AMANDA enters her flat. She goes through the ritualistic routine, exactly the same as normal. She sits down and opens her bag – a brand new pad of paper and pack of envelopes.

SCENE SIXTEEN: LENA'S FLAT, SUMMER – DAY.

LENA is sitting in her flat, MUSIC playing. Five unopened letters lay on the table in front of her.
The PHONE RINGS.
She picks it up. The line is open but there is no-one there. She listens for a second and then slams it down again. She sighs.
The PHONE RINGS again, she grabs it, expecting it to be silent again and says nothing. There is a pause as she waits for the call to cut off before...
GREG speaks on the other end. LENA is sharp and to the point, but relieved to hear his voice.

LENA: Greg?... Of course it's me. Did you phone me a second ago?... Just now?... Maybe you dialled by accident?... Oh, I just wondered. What time are you...? (*Deep disappointment*) Greg!? Can't you cancel it? Well, I've... Alright, I'll come over later.... No, not here. No, I... let me come over to your place again. (*Pause*) Look, I really... Can't you get out of it I really wanted to tell you something. No, I don't want to talk about it now... You might be, but I don't want to tell you over the phone.... No... I need to show you something... No! You..., you haven't been... Have you sent me anything lately?... Anything?... No it's not a hint. No, I'm not pregnant! I've..., someone's been writing to me, and phoning – I think. No I haven't phoned the police. They're letters Greg, that's all. I've been trying to think who it could be, trying to work out who would do this? Maybe it's that kid from the estate I don't know? - the one who stole my mobile last month. He could have got my number from my phone, but... I know I shouldn't have rung him, but .... Yeah, it's probably some joke isn't it? Some big joke. He probably hasn't got anything better to do with his time. No, no I'm fine, they're just letters..., Look I'll see you later.

She puts phone down. She sighs and looks around the room, she is about to get up when the PHONE RINGS. She looks at it but does not answer.
LENA sits, looking at the phone.
The RINGING FADES.

SCENE SEVENTEEN: AMANDA'S FLAT, SUMMER – NIGHT.

CLICKS – LOUDER now as AMANDA tries hard to read her poetry and ignore it. But it becomes unbearable, she turns to the phone, speaking towards it.

AMANDA: Please, I'd like to finish this.

She turns back to the book, but again is drawn to the phone.

AMANDA: Darling please, I really can't... It's not that I don't care, of course I care. Have you any idea how long it takes me to write to you every day?

Again she returns to the book, but again she is distracted.

AMANDA: I..., I don't know what to say. Every time I phone my mouth dries, I can't get the words out, that's why I write, that's' why I tell you everything in the letters... Of course I want to talk to you, I love to hear the sound of your voice, but it scares me somehow: The distance and yet the closeness. (Pause) When we're together it will be different, I promise, then we can talk for hours. It's not you, it's my silly fault, really it is.

She returns to the book for a moment, but looks back, slightly concerned.

AMANDA: Is it him? Has he upset you again? Oh my darling I've told you what you must do. He's no good for you, our love can only truly blossom once you have gotten rid of him. Yes, I know, I know my precious love, but we...

The PHONE RINGS suddenly. AMANDA nearly jumps out of her skin. She composes herself and carefully lifts the receiver.

AMANDA: Hello? (*Then disappointed*) Oh. No, I'm trying to work... Yes mother, well there's a lot of reading to do, you wouldn't understand. It's very difficult when I keep getting interrupted. Well I'm at work all day and... I'm not ignoring you I haven't had time to call... I have, I've been out a lot... I've been out most of the time - I'm seeing someone at the moment. (*Pause*) Well why would you know? I haven't mentioned it because I haven't had a chance to call you... They're not mysterious mother, they're just an ordinary person. And no, you're not going to meet them just yet... Soon,

I don't know, it depends how things work out... Look I really haven't got time to discuss this at the moment, I'm at least two weeks behind on my course work as it is... Yes, I will, I promise, as soon as I get a chance I'll call you. Goodbye.

She puts the phone down. She waits a moment before picking up the book, but only after a few lines the CLICKS start to sound again, LOUDER than before.
She speaks fondly to them.

AMANDA: Believe me you wouldn't want to meet her. She would ask you all sorts of questions... I know you're good with people darling, but I'm not sure she'd understand – you know – about us. (*Her tone changes again to one of concern*). Oh my love, don't be like that, of course I'd like you to meet her. I..., I... Alright. If you insist I will phone you, of course I will, you know I'd do anything for you.

Amanda picks up the phone and starts to dial.

SCENE EIGHTEEN: LENA'S FLAT, SUMMER – NIGHT.

LENA is shouting at GREG off stage.

LENA: (*Off*) ...Well that's just it isn't it! You don't want to do anything for me, because you're too concerned with yourself! Yes you are, you couldn't give a shit about what I need! If you walk away from me Greg Davis you can forget it. I mean it, if you walk away you can fuck off! Fine! If that's the way you want it that's fine, keep walking. Oh, big man, walking away, can't even look at me now? That's it, keep walking. Oh get in your stupid little car and fuck off!

The outer door slams.
LENA enters, accidentally kicking a pile of letters that have built up behind the door in her absence and scattering them across the floor. Most of the letters are in the familiar envelopes sent by AMANDA. She looks at the scattered mail in trepidation. After a short pause she rushes back out of the door.

LENA: (*Off*) Greg? (Pause) Greg!

The PHONE RINGS.
LENA re-enters slowly, cautiously looking over at the phone.
The ANSWERPHONE picks up the call.
We hear the ANSWERPHONE'S outgoing message.

LENA (VO): Hello this is Lena Kern, you can leave me a message, or phone me on my mobile which is 07858 426871, that's 07858 426871. If it's a business call you can try 020 7621 3538, as I pick up my voicemail from the office regularly. Oops, here come the tones.

The TONES sound, they play for quite a while, implying there are a lot of messages. The final TONE sounds before...

GREG (VO): (*TRAFFIC NOISE in background*) Look Lena, I know you're there 'cause I've only just left you. Pick up, pick up Lena. Oh, this is ridiculous. I don't know what's going on here, but I'm not prepared to have the intimate details of our relationship shouted across the street. You knew what the deal was here, we're both busy people Lena, we need space. It's not as if this is some recent development. There is no-one else, OK? (Annoyed) Will you pick up the phone please? I have never stopped you going out and having a good time, because I trust you. And if you can't trust me then, well quite frankly, what is the point of carrying on? You obviously can't even be bothered to pick up the phone, so..., well that says it all really. Call me when you've calmed down, if you want to.

The phone clicks off, the ANSWERPHONE REWINDS.
LENA stands, staring at it.

SCENE NINETEEN: AMANDA'S FLAT, SUMMER – DAY.

AMANDA is on the phone. She is waiting, listening.
Papers and forms of all descriptions are strewn over the floor, as if she has been looking for something. She seems uptight, annoyed.
Her attitude changes as soon as she speaks, to one of pleasantness.

AMANDA: Hello? Yes, I'm sorry, I knew the building but not the extension. Oh, voicemail? Yes, that's great, thank you. (*Pause as she waits for the call to connect, her attitude slips back to the previous state*). Hello?.. Oh.... Yes, this is a message for Greg. Greg, don't you dare ever upset Lena again. You don't even deserve to lick the shit from her shoes you worthless bastard. Thankfully she does have someone who cares for her, she does have someone who will listen to her and take the time treat her with the respect that she deserves. It's just a shame that she's taken this long to let you know.

She puts the phone down in satisfaction.

SCENE TWENTY: LENA'S FLAT, AUTUMN – DAY.

LENA is on the phone to a client.

LENA: ...yes and now everything's waiting for you. No, I'm not getting narky David, I just expect people to be reliable... But this isn't the first time this month is it?... What, the postman's stealing my mail now is he?... So it's done now then?... So, 'if I send a bike over now he can pick it up done', or 'you'd like to add some finishing touches and it may be this afternoon' done?... Now? No, it's your job to make sure your artwork gets to me on time, you can pay for it. All I can say is there's never been a problem with anything sent here before... Fine, then send it to the office in future, I don't really care David, as long as I get it on time, alright?

She puts the phone down.
She picks up the post, there is not that much apart from four or five letters from AMANDA.
LENA looks towards the door, thinking about the postman.
She walks over to the paper bin and goes to throw AMANDA's letters away, but something catches her eye. There is no postmark on her letters. She looks at them and realises they are thicker than they used to be, there is something other than paper inside.
Gingerly LENA takes a letter opener and slices open one of the letters.
She pulls out two pages of writing and a photograph.
She looks at the photograph, concerned deeply by it's subject, then back to the letter. She reads some of the letter. She sits down.
She skims quickly down the page before tearing open another one, again a photograph and two pages of writing, then a third – all the same.
She looks around, unsure of what to do.
She picks up the phone. Her voice is shaking.

LENA: Hello, could I speak to Greg Davis please... Well could you ask him to come out of his meeting for a moment please then Cara?... What call? I haven't been giving my friends his number, anyway what business is it of yours if I had? No, I don't want you to give him a message, I want to speak to him... Yes, I know, you said. Alright, put me through to his voice mail.

As she waits for the connection to his voicemail, she tries to hold back her emotions.

LENA: Hello Greg, it's me. I don't know why you don't get rid of that bitch, she's so rude. Anyway I've got some more of the letters. They..., he's been watching me..., watching us. Heaven knows what's in the ones I've been throwing away. And he knows that too, he knows I've been throwing his letters away. Here, let me read you some of this: '...you looked so beautiful in that red dress, it was a pity that <u>he</u> had to spoil things again. The sooner you are rid of him the better. He's poisoning you against me'. 'Poisoning' Greg. And there's a photograph of us, that night, and others: You and Cara, outside your office, me at the supermarket. The supermarket for Christ's sake. He's put, with the one of you and Cara, '...Much as it breaks my heart to send this, perhaps now you will realise he is no good for you. Your only true happiness, my darling, can be when the two of us are rid of him and only have each other.' What the hell is that supposed to mean Greg? He's obviously some, some nutter. I just don't know what to do, I want to burn them but then, maybe I should keep them in case..., well in case something happens. Please Greg, I need to speak to you. I don't want to be on my own right now. Ring me when you can, please.

She places the phone down and looks at the letters.
She walks around the flat, not really knowing what to do, pulling the curtains tightly, making sure the door is locked etc. as...

AMANDA (*Reading*): '...Your only true happiness, my darling, can be when the two of us are rid of him and only have each other. Only then can we two truly enjoy what I know you have been yearning for. Soon my darling, soon we shall be eternally together.

LENA looks around the flat apprehensively.

SCENE TWENTY-ONE: AMANDA'S FLAT, AUTUMN – MORNING.

AMANDA is getting ready to go out.
The PHONE RINGS.

AMANDA: Hello. (Pleasant) Oh, hello, yes.... Wednesday? No, I'm afraid I can't do Wednesday. Well I'm very busy at the moment.... No, Thursday's no good either. I don't really think I'm going to be able to work any days this week... Oh, yes, yes, I'm still interested. I just have a lot on at the moment, that's all... Would you? Yes, hopefully next week then? Thanks, goodbye.

She puts the phone down and starts to go out, but she returns for her camera.
CLICKS.

AMANDA: Yes my darling I'm coming. Don't worry, I won't miss you.

She turns and exits as the CLICKS get louder and then stop.

SCENE TWENTY-TWO: LENA'S FLAT, AUTUMN – EARLY EVENING.

LENA enters. She goes back to the door and opens it, to see if someone is following her.
Her routine is still there, but is broken periodically as she stops to listen or look out of the window.
Her MESSAGES consist of a few clients and lots of phones being put down without anyone speaking.
We see that in her bag she has some of the letters.
She goes to the window and looks out. She is there for ages, a mirror of AMANDA looking through the peep hole.
LENA puts her music on and tries to relax, but she looks cold and uncomfortable.

SCENE TWENTY-THREE: LENA'S FLAT, AUTUMN – NIGHT.

The stage is empty, it is the middle of the night.
A PHONE rings LOUDLY, but it is unclear whose.
After a few rings LENA enters, in her night clothes. She shuffles over to the phone, still half asleep.
She picks it up.

LENA: Hello?

Silence.

LENA: Hello, who is this?

Silence.
AMANDA has crept on in the darkness and is now holding her own phone.
LENA is about to put the phone down when...

AMANDA: (*Slowly*) It's me.

LENA: Hello?

AMANDA: Hello Lena.

LENA: (*Curious, more than worried*) Who is this?

AMANDA: Don't you recognise my voice?

LENA: Your voice?

AMANDA: It's me my darling.

LENA's eyes widen, as the implication of who she is talking to sinks in.

AMANDA: When the livid morning breaks
You will find no one in my place,
And feel a chill till night is near.

LENA is surprised that it is the voice of a woman.

LENA: (*Disbelieving*) You've been writing to me?

AMANDA: (*Apologetic*) I know. I couldn't bring myself to talk to you again before, I didn't know what to say, in case he... But that's over now, now I have spoken to you things are so much easier, don't you think? No more silly messages, no more hanging up the phone. Now we can talk to our heart's content.

LENA: Who are you?

AMANDA: Lena, darling, don't tease...

LENA: Why are you doing this to me?

AMANDA: It's what you wanted?

LENA: How did you get this number?

AMANDA: You gave it to me, of course...

LENA: The photographs...

AMANDA: I had to let you know I was there for you, your guardian angel, my darling.

LENA: This has to stop, now.

AMANDA: Of course. Now we can be together, now we have each other.

LENA: What are you talking about?

AMANDA: It's what you wanted. You asked me...

LENA: Stop saying that! I don't know who you are, or what you want but this is going to stop now, do you understand?

AMANDA: Lena? Don't be afraid of our love, my darling...

LENA: Don't ring me.

AMANDA: Darling I...

LENA: Don't ring me, don't write to me, do you hear?

AMANDA: Darling? It's what you wanted, it's what you've been asking me to do?

LENA: No, I haven't.

AMANDA: What's wrong? (*Slightly* concerned) Do you want me to come over?

LENA: No! (*Then measured*) Stay away from me.

She slams the phone down, then pulls the plug from the wall. LENA is tense, but strong – she has remained in control. She checks the door is locked and then draws her night clothes up around her, before exiting to the bedroom.

INTERVAL

SCENE TWENTY-FOUR: AMANDA'S FLAT, AUTUMN – EARLY EVENING.

AMANDA walks around her flat, she is on the phone, free and light in tone. She still has piles of papers around, still has the empty glass sitting on the side.

AMANDA: Hello, me again. I'm thinking of going to the Tate this evening, I know you're probably busy but I thought we could meet up for a coffee? Ring me when you get a chance.

She puts the phone down. Almost immediately she picks it up again.

AMANDA: Lena? Are you there? I thought maybe you were in the bath or something before, I'll try your mobile. Speak soon, bye.

She dials again.

AMANDA: Lena. Hello I've left a couple of messages on your home phone, but I've just realised it's Thursday and that's your gym day isn't it? I'll probably, oh no, I'll leave the Tate for another day. But I'll try and see you at the gym. I know it's difficult if you've got friends and clients around, you don't want them thinking you've started a relationship so soon after leaving him. So, never mind we'll keep our distance in public still. I understand fully my darling, so don't let it trouble you. Just seeing you is enough for me and I'm sure you feel the same. Anyway, if you get a chance call me, see you.

She puts the phone down and dials straight away.

AMANDA: Erm, Lena? Just in case you don't get the message I've left on your mobile, I'm not going to the Tate now: I didn't want you to be waiting there for me unnecessarily. I'll try and catch you at the gym, erm... I think I said most of what I wanted to say on the mobile message, so you might want to check that as well. Anyway, love you, bye. Oh, oh, just a minute I was thinking of you today, I was reading this...

She picks up the Baudelaire book and opens it.

AMANDA (Reading): 'O soft enchantress, let me tell the truth
Of all the beauties decking out your youth!
I'll paint the charms for you to see
Of childhood married with maturity...'

She stops reading, listening to the phone impatiently.

AMANDA: Hello? Hello? Oh, I think I've been..., just a minute darling.

She puts the phone down and presses re-dial.

AMANDA: I'm sorry darling I forgot how short these answerphone messages are, they hardly let you say anything at all do they? Don't worry I'll write it down for you instead. I'm a bit busy today, so there'll only be two letters. Please don't think I've forgotten you. I'll see if I can get you a little something to make up for it. So long my precious, I look forward to seeing you later. I must go now, otherwise I'll miss you leaving work. Farewell my love.

She puts the phone down, grabs her coat and rushes out of the door.

SCENE TWENTY-FIVE: LENA'S FLAT, AUTUMN – EARLY EVENING.

LENA enters her flat, she is back in control to an extent. She has decided to ignore the situation until it goes away.
She regimentally goes through her routine. She checks the messages.

ANSWERPHONE (VO): You have sixty-five messages.

LENA presses the button.

ANSWERPHONE (VO): Messages erased.

She flicks through the post, tearing any letters she doesn't recognise, or recognises as Amanda's, and throwing it into the bin.
She puts her MUSIC on and turns on the PC.
She dials out on her mobile, resting it on her ear as she checks the emails. She deletes many of the messages.

LENA: Hi, Alicia? It's Lena. ... I know, I've been busy. I'm fine thanks, how are you? ... Good. I'm just phoning to give you my new mobile number, yes I've upgraded it. ... I know, but I didn't really want to keep the old number. ... Oh great, so I don't even have to tell you what it is, you can transfer it over? ... The wonders of modern technology, eh? ... Oh it is, a total pain, luckily I've had all my numbers converted over to this one, still it gives me a chance to call people I haven't spoken to for a while. ... When? Oh, yes that was when it got stolen, I didn't change the number then though. ... Admirer? Oh, that, yes it was just someone messing around. I have spoken to you since then? ... really? Well, we'll have to make an effort to get together this month, catch up. ... Today? Erm, no, this week's not good. Look I've changed my email address too, so I'm just sending you the new one. ... Got fed up with the old one. ... Next week? Erm..., I'm not sure really. Can I call you? Yeah, you too, bye.

LENA presses the mobile off. She thinks for a moment. She looks at the phone, then over to the bin with all the letters in. She walks over to the bin and takes the letters out again. She starts to look through them.

SCENE TWENTY-SIX: AMANDA'S FLAT, AUTUMN – MORNING.

AMANDA's MUSIC plays, as she sits and composes a letter to LENA.

AMANDA: 'My precious Lena, I am surprised you haven't phoned. It has been nearly two weeks now since your split with him and I had hoped we may have got together, in private at least.
I am worried about you my love, the strain of this public denial is taking it's toll. I try to understand, but please do not torture yourself so. I saw you at the tube station this morning, you are looking ill my love. If the secret of our desire is so hard to bear then perhaps it is time to forget this façade and announce our true feelings to the world? Please do not fear for me, I am stronger than you think. Our love will armour us against the world. And please, do not worry, I have not stopped loving you.
I have waited patiently by the phone, your messages deafen me at times, but to hear your voice it would be worth enduring the sound of a thousand cannons.

She picks up the book and turns to 'I Love You as I Love...'. She copies the text into the letter as she reads.

AMANDA: "I love you as I love the night's high vault
O silent one, o sorrow's lachrymal,
And love you more because you flee from me,
And temptress of my nights, ironically
You seem to hoard the space, to take to you
What separates my arms from heaven's blue.

I climb to the assault, attack the source,
A choir of wormlets pressing towards a corpse,
And cherish your unbending cruelty,
This iciness so beautiful to me."

So, you see, my darling I am prepared to wait for you. I will persist because I know you will come to me soon. In the meantime I will remain patient and steal my images of you at a distance. Until you are ready to be folded into my loving arms.
Your constant and never waning love.
A.'

SCENE TWENTY- SEVEN: AMANDA'S FLAT, AUTUMN – DAY.

The stage is empty.
There is the sound of A KEY TURNING IN A LOCK, although it is not clear who's.
AMANDA enters.
She goes through her routine but half way through there is a KNOCK at the door.
She is thrown slightly by this – no one ever calls at her house. Guardedly she approaches the door. She looks through the spy hole and is pleasantly surprised by what she sees.
She opens the door to reveal LENA standing there.

AMANDA: Please, come in.

AMANDA steps aside and LENA takes one step into the room.

AMANDA: Let me get you something...

She starts to busy herself with 'entertaining' her guest.

LENA: (*Direct*) I know it's you.

AMANDA looks at her, she gives her a puzzled smile.

LENA: It took me a while, but I know now.

AMANDA: What do you mean?

LENA: I know it's you: Who's been sending me the letters, phoning.

AMANDA: But you've always known?

LENA: What?

AMANDA: You've always known it was me? Who else do you think it would be?

LENA: So you're not denying it?

AMANDA: Denying it? Why would I want to do that?

LENA: You've got some nerve.

AMANDA: Lena, darling, I don't know what you mean?

LENA: I'm not here to get annoyed, to scream and shout. I'm just here to tell you that I know it's you now and if you don't stop then I'll be forced to contact the police.

AMANDA: What for?

LENA: What for? What do you think? Harassment.

AMANDA is surprised by the allegation.

AMANDA: But darling...

LENA: Don't keep calling me that! I don't put up with it from men and I'm certainly not going to put up with it from you. Now I appreciate your help, all those months ago, but please listen to me – this has to stop. I don't even know you, I can't even remember your name.

AMANDA: Don't be ridiculous...

LENA: I'm not the one who's being ridiculous...

AMANDA: It's me, Amanda. We're alone here, you don't have to pretend...

LENA: Look, Amanda, I don't know why you chose me...

AMANDA: But I didn't?

LENA stops. She looks at AMANDA.

AMANDA: How could I have? (*Pause*) I didn't know anything about you, not then. You came to me...

LENA: I had my phone stolen!

AMANDA: Then perhaps fate brought us together, brought you to me, but it was you who initiated it all after that. I would never have dreamed of it, if you hadn't been so insistent. I must admit, to my shame, I tried to ignore it, God knows I tried. But thankfully you gave me strength, you were too persistent my love.

LENA: (*Disbelief*) How, exactly did I initiate it?

AMANDA: Well you..., you touched me, of course.

LENA: What are you talking about?

AMANDA: You touched me. Right where you are standing now my darling, that was your signal.

LENA: I told you not to call me that...

AMANDA: You touched me, like this...

She reaches forward and touches LENA's arm, as she flinches away.

AMANDA: ...And you said 'Look out for yourself my precious love'. And then you gave me that look, that look which begged me to contact you, to find you, to be with you.

LENA: I didn't say that.

AMANDA: Of course you did my love.

LENA: I didn't.

LENA cannot believe what she is hearing. She paces a few steps around the flat as...

LENA: (*Trying to remain composed*) I'm sorry if you think I gave you some indication that I was interested in you but I'm not. I'm not interested in you Amanda. Please believe me. All these phone calls and letters, its..., it's not normal.

AMANDA: Of course it's not normal. Do you think all this is normal? (*Indicating the piles of letters and post*) Lena, my love, it's an obsession. An obsession that only we two can know, that our love has created.

LENA: I don't love you!

AMANDA just looks at her, lovingly.

LENA: (*She goes to touch her, but then thinks better of it*). It's not healthy Amanda, you obviously need help.

AMANDA: Isn't that just like you, to think of me before yourself.

LENA: No it's not like me. You don't know anything about me.

AMANDA: I know everything about you my darling, what do you think I spend my time doing? To know you is to love you...

LENA: I don't want you to know me, I just want you to leave me alone. I can't cope with it anymore, if you truly felt anything for me you'd stop this nonsense right now and get on with your life.

AMANDA: This is my life. You are my life.

LENA: No, I'm not! What is it going to take to make you understand that?

Looking at the stack of letters on the side, LENA notices that some of them are the torn letters that she has been putting in the bin.

LENA: (*Apprehensively*) What's this?

She pulls out some of the letters, as she does so she sees other letters addressed to her that she has never seen.

LENA: (*Slightly annoyed*) What are these?

She picks a stack of them up and starts to sift through.

LENA: I threw these away... (*Continuing to sift*)

AMANDA: I'm sure you didn't mean to...

LENA: And this..., this is my post. What are you doing with my post?

AMANDA: (*Cheerful*) Your postman gives it to me, he's always there at about seven-thirty. Sometimes he even calls me 'Miss Kern'. I think it's just his little joke, as we're not alike at all to look at are we? Secretly I think he knows – about us...

LENA: You've been stealing my mail!

AMANDA: Not stealing it my darling. He gives it to me and I pass it on to you, unless there's something I'm not sure about and then...

LENA: (*Waving a large envelope at* her) I nearly lost a contract over this artwork!

AMANDA: I thought it might be a gift...

LENA: This is my private stuff! And..., you've been going through my rubbish haven't you? My paper rubbish, these are my old bills, and my letters – what the hell do you think you're doing?

AMANDA: I just wanted to keep up with what you were doing...

LENA: This is insane! What else have you got of mine...?

AMANDA: You said you'd thrown it away...

LENA: Not for you to pick up! For Christ's sake Amanda what do you think you're doing here? This has to stop, do you hear me? I'm not putting up with it any longer. No one should have to put up with this! What is it you hope to achieve? Do you expect me to love you? Do you really expect me to love you!? How can you expect me to even like you? Even if I was interested in other women, which incidentally I'm not, why would I be interested in you! You're a fucking fruit loop!! I don't want anything to do with you, I never have and I never will. So whatever it is you thought I'd said, whatever it is you thought I'd done, forget it. Just leave me alone! Could I be any clearer? Could I be any clearer!?

AMANDA stands looking at her, her expression has not changed throughout the whole verbal assault.
LENA, having achieved no response, turns to leave.
She turns back.

LENA: And don't think you can intimidate me with all this shit! With your letters and your phone calls... And don't you dare set foot anywhere near me or my flat ever again, do you understand?

LENA turns and slams the door as she exits, taking the papers with her.
AMANDA stands motionless, emotionless.
LENA's FOOTSTEPS can be heard loudly as she walks away and back to her own flat as...
AMANDA walks over to the sofa and takes out a pen and her pad as...

SCENE TWENTY-EIGHT: LENA'S FLAT/AMANDA'S FLAT, WINTER – LATER THAT DAY.

The FOOTSTEPS stop.
LENA enters her flat, closes the door and takes the letters etc. straight to the non-recyclable bin bag and stuffs them in.
She stands for a while, composed, fuming, before she collapses in a heap of tears.
While she is sobbing AMANDA starts to write...

AMANDA: 'It was so lovely to see you today. I knew you'd come eventually, I'm sorry I ever doubted you my love. I can understand why you wanted to collect the letters: Now he's gone there is no reason to hide anything anymore. It would be nice perhaps if you could send me a little trinket, to remember you by when we can't be together. Something small? I still have the glass that you first sipped from, unwashed and preserved, but something I could keep with me always – close to my heart – would truly show how much you loved me. I enjoyed your little game of pretending to forget my name, as if you don't repeat it a thousand times in your sleep as I do?...'

AMANDA continues to write as...
LENA's PHONE RINGS LOUDLY.
LENA goes to the answerphone and turns it off, so that she doesn't have to hear the message.
Still the PHONE RINGS.
She tries to ignore it. She covers her ears with her hands but the RINGING GROWS LOUDER.
Eventually she cannot stand it anymore and picks it up.

LENA: Leave me alone!

The voice at the other end is not AMANDA, she comes to her senses before they put the phone down.

LENA: Greg? Greg, thank goodness. I'm going out of my mind. ... Can you come over? ... Where? ... Well what are you doing there? You can't be I, I need you here. ... I know, I know what I said but please, she's, she's... Amanda. Yes, I thought it was, but it's a woman. ... Amanda – the one who's house I went to when my phone was stolen. ... She what? Phoned you? Of course I didn't give her the number... Yes. ... Nothing, I, I don't know I can't remember. ... Of course I didn't. Greg, I'd know if I was leading her on. ... Nothing, a touch, something, I don't know. Please, you have to come over as soon as you get back to England. ... I expect you to help me... No, I haven't called the police. ... And say what? ... What do you mean 'if something happens'? ... Like what? Greg you're frightening me. ... Ten days? ... Can't you...? Alright, alright, I'm sorry. Ten days. No, I've changed the number, I'll phone you. ... Yes, I'll try and get the calls barred. ... No, I won't contact her.

She puts the phone down and unplugs it from the wall.
LENA huddles in the corner of the room. She slowly collapses, as her world has done. She crouches into the foetal position, exhausted by her emotions she falls asleep as...
AMANDA finishes writing her letter and puts it in an envelope, which she seals with a kiss. She crosses the room and puts it on the floor at LENA's door. On the way back she kisses her hand and gently presses it to LENA's head as she passes.

SCENE TWENTY-NINE: LENA'S FLAT, WINTER – EARLY MORNING.

LENA wakes.
She looks at the time and crosses to the door.
She sees the letter and stops dead in her tracks.
All the fear, all the anger from the previous day rushes back.
She snatches up the letter and tears it open. After reading the first few lines, trembling with disbelief she screws it up in the palm of her hand and clenches her fists in frustration.
She stuffs the letter back into the envelope and scrawls across the front 'RETURN TO SENDER'.
Manically she Selotapes the letter shut and scribbles out her own address, writing AMANDA's in its place.
She picks up the phone and dials 192.

LENA: Hello, I wonder if you could help me, I need a phone number? ... Yes, the address? It's Amanda, erm, I can't remember her surname but the address is 87 Omni House, Alberta Estate, Kennington. ... London, yes. ... Ex-directory? But I need to... Well it is an emergency, couldn't you...? I see, no, thank you.

She puts the phone down, thinks for a moment and then picks it up and dials.

LENA: Hello, it's Lena here. I'm just leaving a message to say that I won't be able to make it in to work today. I have to sort something out – a personal matter – hopefully I'll be in, well of course I'll be in, tomorrow. Thanks.

She puts the phone down, grabs her keys and exits quickly with the letter, determined to get rid of it.

SCENE THIRTY: AMANDA'S FLAT, WINTER, TWO DAYS LATER – DAY.

AMANDA has LENA's rubbish bag all over her floor, she has been sifting through it. Among it is some 'ready meals' packaging.
She sits writing...

AMANDA: 'Thank you for your reply to my last letter. How thoughtful to return my own correspondence to me, as a keepsake – returning my love for you with equal measure. I noticed you were not at work yesterday, I hope you are feeling alright, it's unlike you to miss a day. I think Andrew was at a complete loss at what to do, you really do hold things together there...'

There is a KNOCK at the door.
AMANDA stops. She glances over to the door.
She puts her writing things down and walks over to the spy hole, glancing back at the rubbish strewn over the floor.
She looks through the spy hole. She is taken back slightly.
Methodically she slides the chain onto the door and opens it a crack, looking round it at the person on the other side, shielding the room from view.

AMANDA: Yes, can I help you officer? ... Lena, yes of course I know her, is she alright? ... Oh, thank goodness. ... No, I'd rather you didn't come in, it's a bit of a mess at the moment. ... Lena? Well, why would she say that? ... Yes I have seen her, she popped round the other day. ... Yes, well, you know... She? ... I'm sorry I really don't know why. She contacts me all the time and then, well she's so insistent that I ring, if you knew her you'd understand. ... Always, yes. She always contacts me first. ... I write to her yes, all the time. Just silly things, you know, love letters I suppose, chat. ... Distress? Oh, the poor dear, I tell her all the time, she's working too hard. She doesn't eat properly I'm sure, all these ready meals she's been having lately. It's probably some silly game she's thought up. If you only knew her... I'm afraid she's been wasting your time. I'm ever so sorry. Please, don't blame her, it's never happened before. ... Yes, I've been seeing her for several months now... Oh yes, she didn't mention it? Well, there we are then, some silly game. ... Yes, I'm sorry officer. I will, I'll tell her. Goodbye.

AMANDA gently closes the door.
She picks up the phone as...

SCENE THIRTY-ONE: LENA'S FLAT/AMANDA'S FLAT, WINTER – DAY.

FADE UP ON LENA's CD as it plays loudly in her flat. The PHONE RINGS, she answers it straight away.

LENA: Hello.

AMANDA: Lena, did you send the police round to my flat?

LENA: (*Deflated*) Yes, yes I did.

AMANDA: Well why did you do that?

LENA: I'm not talking to you Amanda.

She goes to put the phone down.

AMANDA: But, what have I done?

LENA: I'm going to put the phone down now.

AMANDA: No, wait. Lena, tell me what I've done?

LENA: Are you joking? You must be joking.

AMANDA: Why would I joke about something so serious? Tell me what I've done to upset you my precious? I've tried to show my love for you my darling, what else can I do?

LENA: I don't want you to love me...

AMANDA: (*Slightly perplexed*) The keepsake you sent me back, why would you do that if you didn't want me to love you, if you didn't love me?

LENA: Amanda...

AMANDA: And your constant messages, begging me to call...

LENA: Amanda, you're living in a fantasy world...

AMANDA: (*Denial*) No. You wanted me. You gave me a sign...

LENA: I touched your arm, I did it without thinking, I probably do it all the time.

AMANDA: No. Not like that, not that way, it was a sign, a sign of love...

LENA: It meant nothing...

AMANDA: Have you found someone else? Tell me you haven't found anyone else?

LENA: I don't need to listen to this.

AMANDA: Who is it? Is it someone at work? I know it's no-one at work...

LENA: Look, Amanda, I'm going to get a restraining order put on you and you are not going to be able to come near me and you are not going to be able to contact me.

AMANDA: But why...?

LENA: Because I hate you and I don't want you anywhere near me.

AMANDA: How can you say that?

LENA: Because it's true.

AMANDA: It's not true my darling.

LENA: Why won't you listen to me?

AMANDA: I love you.

LENA: Then you'd better think about whether it's worth going to jail for.

Pause.

AMANDA: Of course it would be.

Beat.

LENA: Listen to yourself. Just listen to what you're saying, how can it be worth it?

AMANDA: If it would prove my love for you...

LENA: How? How would that prove you loved me?

AMANDA: Because I am prepared to sacrifice everything for you. When Cupid...

LENA: Fuck Cupid! Amanda this is realty. If you love me, if you really love me, then prove it. Prove it just by leaving me alone.

AMANDA: How can I leave you alone, when we mean so much to each other?

LENA: There is nothing between us Amanda, nothing.

AMANDA: How can you say that, when you know it's not true? You just said you wanted me to prove my love to you? Lena what's wrong with you?

LENA: You! You are what's wrong with me! You have fucked me up. I can't talk to people any more, I can't even look at people, smile at them, in case they read some unintentional meaning into it. You are destroying me. How can that be love? How can it be love? I wish you'd drop dead!

AMANDA: Lena it's hard to talk with that music blaring in the background.

LENA: I don't want to talk to you.

AMANDA: Lena, I'm trying to talk to you... Lena darling...

LENA: I've told you not to call me that.

AMANDA: Lena please...

LENA TURNS UP THE MUSIC and holds the receiver to the speaker.

AMANDA: Lena? Lena!

She holds the phone away from her ear slightly.

AMANDA: Lena, turn it down. Lena please. Lena! Alright, fine. I think you've made your point. If you don't want to talk to me then that's fine. You know where I am, don't expect me to call you back.

AMANDA slams the phone down.
She is clearly upset by the whole thing, she looks at the phone for a while, before wiping her eyes and moving away. She paces the flat as...
LENA listens to the phone. She realizes AMANDA has gone. She turns the music down, slightly pleased with herself. She puts the phone down.
LENA turns the MUSIC OFF.
She stands and looks at the phone. For a few moments both of them move around their own space, unsure of what to do, expecting the phone to ring.
LENA is the first to move to the phone, she sits down and dials. AMANDA resists as long as she can as...

LENA: ...WPC Rowlings? Yes, she's phoned me again, just now. Well of course I didn't record the conversation. ... But you've spoken to her, you know what she's like? Won't there be some record of the call? ... But she phones thirty or forty times a day sometimes, surely that's proof enough? ... No, I've thrown them away. No, I've deleted them. Evidence? She's been stealing my rubbish. ... No, I don't have any of the letters or emails. ... I can't... OK, I'll try and keep a record. ... But that means that she'll... Well didn't you warn her? I told you what she's been doing... Alright, I'm sorry. So, once she's been told she is causing me distress, if she continues... I see. I would have thought it was obvious... Yes, I understand...

LENA continues the conversation in silence as...
AMANDA has dialled out, she waits as...

BT RESPONSE (VO): (*Three pips*) Please hold the line, the person you are calling knows you are waiting. (*Three pips*) Please hold the line, the person you are calling knows you are waiting. (*Three pips*) Please hold the line the person you are calling knows you are waiting.

LENA: ...That's probably her now.

BT RESPONSE (VO): Sorry, please try later.

They both put the phone down. As AMANDA dials another number LENA takes the phone plug out of the wall.

VODAPHONE RESPONSE (VO): The number you have called is not recognised, please check the number. If you need help call the operator on 100 from your mobile.

AMANDA: I don't have a mobile.

AMANDA puts the phone down. She dials LENA again. LOUD RING TONE (FROM CALLERS PERSPECTIVE). Oblivious to the call (as her phone is disconnected) LENA sits down with a small pad and starts to make a list.

AMANDA: (*Half crying)* Oh my darling, I'm sorry, I'm so sorry. I didn't mean those things I said. Please forgive me darling, I never meant to hurt you...

RING TONE FADES, as LENA writes and AMANDA waits for an answer.

SCENE THIRTY-TWO: AMANDA'S FLAT, WINTER - DAY.

AMANDA sits on the floor of her flat.
Her MUSIC IS PLAYING LOUDLY.
She is carefully and lovingly wrapping a CD of the recording she is listening to. She places a card inside and then encloses the whole thing neatly into a Jiffy bag.
She writes LENA's address on the front and kisses the packet.
She stands, picks up her coat and the packet and exits.

SCENE THIRTY-THREE: LENA'S FLAT/AMANDA'S FLAT, WINTER – DAY.

LENA enters. She is carrying a large lined hardback book, a desk diary, a stack of plastic folders and the package from AMANDA.
The curtains to the flat are drawn.
She throws the package into a box, unopened.
She places the other things down and checks her messages.

ANSWERPHONE (VO): You have seventy-two messages.

LENA presses the button, but does not erase the messages.
She picks up the post and places it on the table. She methodically sorts it into piles.
She is on autopilot, blinkered.
The PHONE RINGS but she does not respond, she carries on sorting the post.
As it CONTINUES RINGING she picks up the diary and opens it.
Taking a ruler she draws lines down the pages, making five or six columns.
The PHONE STOPS RINGING, but still she has no reaction.
At the top of each column she writes a heading as...
The PHONE RINGS AGAIN.
She continues until she has finished, she looks at the page, she is pleased with the result. She picks up the phone.

LENA: (*Flatly*) Hello. ... Oh, hello Patrick. Yes, I'm afraid I'm a bit busy at the moment, can I call you back? ... Soon, yes. I don't know when.

She puts the phone down, still preoccupied with the task at hand.
She turns on the PC.
She goes to the answerphone, opens the book and presses the button.

ANSWERPHONE (VO): You have seventy-two messages.

LENA takes the pen and opens the book, ready to write.
The PHONE RINGS.
She clicks the answerphone off and waits a moment.
She answers the phone.

LENA: (*As before*) Hello.

As soon as she realises who it is she places the receiver on the table, keeping the line open. She makes an entry into the book, logging time, duration etc.as...

AMANDA: Lena, darling it's me. I've left you a few messages already. You haven't been at work again today. Where did you get to my darling? I was up so early, I don't know how I missed you. I called round to drop off a little something, hopefully you've had a chance to listen to it. I noticed your curtains are drawn again today, I didn't like to knock in case I disturbed you. Lena, are you there my precious? Lena, why won't you talk to me? Lena I can't bear this silence, don't ignore me my darling, please.

Silence.
Regretfully AMANDA puts the phone down.
LENA picks up the receiver and listens – the line is dead. She places it back onto the phone cradle.
AMANDA has already dialled and it RINGS straight away.
It KEEPS RINGING as...
LENA looks over at the curtains. She walks over and pulls them firmly shut, so no-one can see in.
AMANDA puts the phone down, it STOPS RINGING.
LENA returns to look at the PC. She checks the emails.
As she looks down the screen she opens the book on another page and writes in it as...
AMANDA dials again.
The PHONE RINGS constantly as...
LENA turns the book back to the 'telephone calls' page.
She picks up the telephone.

LENA: Hello.

SCENE THIRTY-FOUR: AMANDA'S FLAT, WINTER – EARLY EVENING.

AMANDA is on the phone.

AMANDA: ...She did give me her new mobile number, but heaven knows what I did with it... It is an emergency, can't you just... Not even this once? I told you, Amanda, Amanda Judd. She does have my number, yes. Please, make sure you do. Tell her it's important.

AMANDA puts the phone down, she's at a total loss, she has been cut off from LENA.
She takes out her writing pad and starts to write a letter, but she finds it difficult to concentrate. She opens her poetry book for inspiration, but it is no help. She puts the pad and pen down.

AMANDA: (*To herself*) I have to see you my darling I..., you don't go out any more it's difficult to know... Perhaps I need to...? If I could actually see you, face to face but... Oh, my darling why do you make things so difficult for us, you're fighting me all the time, if only you'd submit...

She thinks for a moment, then goes and gets a piece of paper from the side. She dials the number.

AMANDA: Greg Davis please. Thank you.

She waits while the call connects.

AMANDA: You bastard, what have you been saying to her? ... Don't give me that, you know who it is. She's stopped my calls to her home phone and her mobile, no-one at work will let me speak to her. ... Why has she done this? ... What would you know about it? What do you think you know about anything? ... We love each other. Can't you get that through your thick head? ... I don't expect you to understand, how could you? ... She does want to see me, but she can't because people like you keep interfering. Why can't you leave us alone? You're just jealous because what we have is so special. ... Do you think I care? Do you think I care what you or anyone else does to me? It's Lena that I care about, and perhaps if you had done a little bit more she wouldn't have chosen me over you.

She puts the phone down and in frustration throws it across the room.
She calms herself, then picks up her coat. She puts it on and checks the pockets for change.
AMANDA exits.

SCENE THIRTY-FIVE: LENA'S FLAT, WINTER – EVENING.

LENA is in her flat, she is sorting through the letters, emails and phone messages. She is logging everything into the book. Letters are placed in the plastic folders. There is a large box of things, including unopened gifts, all from AMANDA. Her diary has now become a record book of contact from AMANDA it is neat and ordered. Her mobile phone is on the table with the battery removed.
There is a recorder set by the phone.
The PHONE RINGS LOUDLY. Routinely LENA gets her things ready, and switches on the recorder which SHUFFLES AND CLICKS (similar in sound to the 'clicks' AMANDA hears).
LENA picks up the phone, she answers flatly, with no emotion whatsoever.

LENA: Hello.

AMANDA (VO): Lena, darling it's me. I'm phoning you from a phone box again because there's something wrong with my phone still. I can't get through to you.

As she continues LENA places the receiver down on the table and starts to write in the diary, she listens but does not respond, other than writing details of time, content, duration etc. in the diary.

AMANDA (VO) (Continued): ...It's very difficult for me at the moment my love, as they've said I mustn't see you. Why must we all abide by these silly rules? Surely our love is greater than that? I know it's not your fault, but it's so frustrating knowing that you are there, longing for me to be with you and yet I cannot come to you. (*Then continuing as...*)

As she is talking LENA walks over to the window. She pulls the curtain back, just enough to see out. She returns to the table and puts the battery into her mobile. She dials.

AMANDA (VO) (Continuing): ...Be comforted, my darling, that I am not far away. How could I ever be distanced from you emotionally or physically? We have a special bond, you and I. We are destined and obligated to be together: To live as one, regardless of what obstacles are cast in our way. There is nothing that nature or mankind could do to crack the forging of our hearts.
'Oh Beauty! Do you visit from the sky
Or the abyss? Infernal and divine,

Your gaze bestows both kindness and crimes,
So it is said you act on us like wine.

Your eye contains the evening and the dawn;
You pour out odours like an evening storm;
Your kiss is potion from an ancient jar,
That can make heroes cold and children warm.

Are you of heaven or of the nether world?
Charmed Destiny, your pet, attends your walk;
You scatter joys and sorrows at your whim,
And govern all, and answer no man's call.
...'

LENA speaks as AMANDA's VOICE CONTINUES.

LENA: (*Whispering*) Hello. It's Lena Kern. She's here again, yes the phone box over the road...

AMANDA; (*Continuing under LENA's actions and words and fading out as her speech trails off*)
'...Beauty, you walk on corpses, mocking them;
Horror is charming as your other gems,
And Murder is a trinket dancing there
Lovingly on your naked belly's skin.

You are a candle where the mayfly dies
In flames, blessing this fire's deadly bloom.
The panting lover bending to his love
Looks like a dying man who strokes his tomb.

What difference, then, from heaven or from hell,
O Beauty, monstrous in simplicity?
If eye, smile, step can open me the way
To find unknown, sublime infinity?

Angel or siren, spirit, I don't care,
As long as velvet eyes and perfumed head
And glimmering motions, o my queen, can make
The world less dreadful, and the time less dead.'

As the speeches fade...
There is the LOUD CRASH OF A CELL DOOR CLOSING.

SCENE THIRTY-SIX: AMANDA'S FLAT, WINTER – NIGHT.

A single spotlight snaps on, revealing AMANDA standing alone facing the audience.

AMANDA: So this is how they intend to keep me away from you? To lock me up? My heart is locked into my breast, caged within my ribs but still it can reach out to you. They can keep me here as long as they like - until you come to your senses, while these four milligrams of Pimozide are designed to keep me from mine. In the mean time I am comforted by the fact that you will be thinking of me. You may not be thinking good thoughts, but you will be thinking of me. Each one of these tablets takes me further from my yearning to be by your side, but I know, deep down it will never stop.

SCENE THIRTY-SEVEN: LENA'S FLAT, SPRING – LATE AFTERNOON.

LENA enters her flat carrying some shopping. She is talking on her mobile. Her tone is lighter now, the burden of the constant attention lifted, but she is still not back to her old self. Actions, routines and speech are all subdued and tarnished by the whole affair.

LENA: ...Apparently, yes. They've put her on some antipsychotic drugs and they seem to be working. I haven't heard a thing for months now. No, she never was violent. In some ways I feel sorry for her, I'd still like to talk to her, draw a line under it now she's OK. But they've advised me not to. ... Me? Oh yes, I'm fine. No, I haven't gone back to work yet but, you know, I'm taking each day as it comes. ... I don't think so, not full time. I keep myself to myself now really. ... Greg's? Yes, I got an invite, are you going? No, it was nice of him to ask though. ... Yes, I'd like that, we should get together - when I'm up to it. I'll ring you. Thanks Alicia.

She switches off the mobile and takes the battery out.
LENA goes through her routine, which now includes additions since the incident – like double checking the door and pulling the curtains tight shut.
LENA pours herself and drink and puts on the CD player.
SHOSTAKOVICH plays.
LENA sits, a shadow of her former self, still slightly un-nerved.
AMANDA, who has been sitting in silence all this time, takes the small bottle of drugs and unscrews the cap. She holds up the bottle and tips the tablets onto the floor
They both look out to the audience.

AMANDA: What is love? Love is an affliction. It's something that catches you off guard, like a barbed hook, hiding in the murky waters. It's often one sided, or maybe it just seems that way. I don't think anyone can force you to love them, it just happens. It's such a bizarre concept, this 'mystical' attachment. It screws you up, definitely, there are far too many distractions in life. That's why you need to stay in control, that's essential I think - focus on what's important. Life is too short to let anything cloud your vision, so you have to keep your head, keep reminding yourself of your goals. Without that you're lost – a victim of your own emotions.

LENA: Love is obsessive. It envelops you, consuming your whole life. There's no choice: You fall in to this fast flowing river, carried along, rushing past while life on the shady banks is a blur of mundane pointless tasks. It's all there is. Everything that's gone before is swept away in the torrent of emotion. It occupies every waking hour. While you might try to ignore it, fight it, reason with it... It's there, clawing at the door, waiting for you to discover that there is nothing as strong, nothing as enduring, nothing as overwhelming. And when you're struck, struck by that poison tipped arrow, well it's hopeless. You can't fight that: Submission is the only choice. That's the truth of it.

PHONE RINGS, fade as...
Fade to black.

Other Plays by the same author include:

THE THIEFTAKER

PEOPLE IN GLASS HOUSES

SMOKE

BOOM

THE SNOW QUEEN

WORLDS APART

THE LITTLE MERMAID

1001 ARABIAN NIGHTS

CLARA AND THE NUTCRACKER

DARREN RAPIER

Darren Rapier trained at Rose Bruford College, graduating in 1995 with a degree in writing. He has written for film, television and theatre. Plays include *The Thieftaker,* about the first real gangster in early Eighteenth Century London; *People in Glass Houses*, a futuristic absurd comedy; *Smoke*, a play with music, about the railway 'improvements' and clearances of 1863; *Boom*, a community play set in 1936, about the housing boom in the South East; *Extensions of Love*, about one woman's obsession with another and *Worlds Apart*, set in India and the UK. Adaptations for children have included *The Snow Queen, The Little Mermaid, 1001 Arabian Nights* and *Clara and the Nutcracker.* Short plays include *The Gallery,* and the ten minute musical *Dying for a Kipp* at Greenwich Theatre. In 2007 he wrote and co-directed *Payback* for Greenwich and Lewisham Young Peoples' Theatre and *Departures* for the National Youth Theatre. He has written and directed two short films *It Is* and *The Race,* is a writer on *Doctors* for the BBC and has two feature films in development. Darren has been short listed for the Carl Forman Award at BAFTA, is a selected short film writer for TAPS and was a finalists in the BBC Talent Television Drama initiative in 2002. His radio play *Vital Statistics* was part of BBC Radio Drama/Hampstead Theatre's 'Stages of Sound' 2006. Darren is also Artistic Director of *Spanner in the Works,* who run drama based workshops in schools, hospitals and museums and a freelance drama trainer and facilitator.

www.ingramcontent.com/pod-product-compliance
Ingram Content Group UK Ltd.
Pitfield, Milton Keynes, MK11 3LW, UK
UKHW021009200726
13857UKWH00004B/1355